Samuel French Acting Edition

W9-ARZ-382

The Elaborate Entrance of Chad Deity

by Kristoffer Diaz

SAMUELFRENCH.COM   SAMUELFRENCH.CO.UK

ISBN 978-0-573-69967-2

www.SamuelFrench.com
www.SamuelFrench.co.uk

FOR PRODUCTION ENQUIRIES

UNITED STATES AND CANADA
Info@SamuelFrench.com
1-866-598-8449

UNITED KINGDOM AND EUROPE
Plays@SamuelFrench.co.uk
020-7255-4302

Each title is subject to availability from Samuel French, depending upon country of performance. Please be aware that *THE ELABORATE ENTRANCE OF CHAD DEITY* may not be licensed by Samuel French in your territory. Professional and amateur producers should contact the nearest Samuel French office or licensing partner to verify availability.

For all enquiries regarding motion picture, television, and other media rights, please contact Samuel French.

MUSIC USE NOTE

Licensees are solely responsible for obtaining formal written permission from copyright owners to use copyrighted music in the performance of this play and are strongly cautioned to do so. If no such permission is obtained by the licensee, then the licensee must use only original music that the licensee owns and controls. Licensees are solely responsible and liable for all music clearances and shall indemnify the copyright owners of the play(s) and their licensing agent, Samuel French, against any costs, expenses, losses and liabilities arising from the use of music by licensees. Please contact the appropriate music licensing authority in your territory for the rights to any incidental music.

IMPORTANT BILLING AND CREDIT REQUIREMENTS

If you have obtained performance rights to this title, please refer to your licensing agreement for important billing and credit requirements.

THE ELABORATE ENTRANCE OF CHAD DEITY was first produced by Victory Gardens in Chicago, IL on September 25, 2009. The performance was directed by Edward Torres, with sets by Brian Sidney Bembridge, costumes by Christine Pascual, lighting by Jessie Klug, sound by Mikhail Fiskel, projections by John Boesche, props by D.J. Reed, fight direction by David Wooley, and dramaturgy by Erica L. Weiss. The Production Stage Manager was Tina M. Jach. The cast was as follows:

VIGNESHWAR PADUAR	Usman Ally
CHAD DEITY	Lamal Angelo Bolden
MACEDONIO GUERRA	Desmin Borges
EVERETT K. OLSON/RING ANNOUNCER	James Krag
JOE JABRONI/BILL HEARTLAND/OLD GLORY	Christian Litke

THE ELABORATE ENTRANCE OF CHAD DEITY was subsequently produced by 2econd Stage Theatre (Carole Rothman, Artistic Director) in New York City on May 20, 2010. The performance was directed by Edward Torres, with sets by Brian Sidney Bembridge, costumes by Christine Pascual, lighting by Jessie Klug, sound by Mikhail Fiskel, projections by Peter Nigrini, and fight direction by David Wooley. The Production Stage Manager was Roy Harris. The cast was as follows:

VIGNESHWAR PADUAR	Usman Ally
CHAD DEITY	Terence Archie
MACEDONIO GUERRA	Desmin Borges
EVERETT K. OLSON/RING ANNOUNCER	Michael T. Weiss
JOE JABRONI/BILL HEARTLAND/OLD GLORY	Christian Litke

CHARACTERS

MACEDONIO GUERRA (also known as **THE MACE**) – A Puerto Rican professional wrestler. Good at what he does, undersized, our hero.

EVERETT K. OLSON (also known as **EKO**) – The Caucasian owner of THE Wrestling. Brash, confident, ostensibly our villain.

CHAD DEITY (also known as **CHAD DEITY**) – The African-American champion of THE Wrestling. Confident, handsome, not a very good wrestler.

VIGNESHWAR PADUAR (also known as **VP**) – A young Indian-American Brooklynite. Charismatic, natural, effortless.

THE BAD GUY – A non-descript professional wrestler (non-speaking; also plays **BILLY HEARTLAND** and **OLD GLORY**).

AUTHOR'S NOTES

A NOTE ON WRESTLING ENTRANCES

I've given specific ideas for the wrestling entrances of some of the characters (particularly Chad Deity) – directors and design teams should, of course, feel free to adapt the entrances according to their own capabilities. The important thing to remember: the size, expense, and spectacle of a wrestler's entrance all speak volumes about his role in the company.

For good examples of what we're talking about here, try to track down Hulk Hogan's Real American entrance, Triple H's *Time to Play The Game* entrance, any of The Rock's entrances, Ric Flair's classic *Thus Spake Zarathustra* entrances, Sandman's *Enter Sandman* entrance, and Goldberg's pyro-filled entrance, among others.

A NOTE ON WRESTLING PROMOS

The wrestling promo is a lot like the sideline interview in legit sports, often without the sideline interviewer. Intense, humorous, or somewhere in-between, the subtext of every promo (and usually the overt text) is (a) I am better than you, and (b) I'm more of a real man than you. For good examples, see the work of Ric Flair, Dusty Rhodes, The Rock, Mick Foley, Stone Cold Steve Austin, and Chris Jericho, among others. For scary intensity, check out Jake "The Snake" Roberts or Taz (ECW days, not WWF). For Chad Deity and other over-the-top, cartoon style promos, see the work of Hulk Hogan, The Ultimate Warrior, Randy Savage, and Scott Steiner.

A NOTE ON THE RING ANNOUNCER

Howard Finkle (of the WWF) is the greatest of all-time. See also Michael Buffer.

A NOTE ON WRESTLING MOVES

Certain moves are mentioned and referenced in this play. Not all versions of these moves are created equal.

Powerbomb: Look at guys like Sid Vicious, Vader, or Brock Lesnar. Batista did a fancier version. There are many variations on the power-bomb. You're probably looking for the simplest one.

Superkick: Many wrestlers include the superkick in their arsenal, but the undisputed epitome of the superkick is Shawn Michaels' "Sweet Chin Music."

A NOTE ON WRESTLING STEREOTYPES

Most of the classic and truly offensive ones are from the WWF/WWE, largely in the eighties and nineties. Some names to check out for reference: Akeem, The African Dream; Saba Simba; The Wild Samoans; The Iron Sheik and Nikolai Volkoff; and of course, Muhammad Hassan and his sidekick Daivari.

A NOTE ON WRESTLING

It is vitally important – VITALLY – that any wrestling or wrestling moves that are used in the course of the play are indeed wrestling moves and not stage combat. There is a subtle but massively important difference. A wrestling technical advisor would be a great person to have on the artistic team.

AND FINALLY...A NOTE ON THE POWERBOMB

The powerbomb is difficult and dangerous, even for professionals. Be prepared to spend time figuring out the best way to handle those sections. You might have to be creative.

For real. Take it seriously.

ACT ONE

(We hear the ringside bell.)

EKO. *(as Ring Announcer)* The following contest is scheduled for one fall with a one hour time limit. Introducing first, already in the ring because he's not enough of a star to warrant his own elaborate entrance, hailing from Parts Unknown because we can't be bothered to come up with a better hometown for him, weighing in at…well, I'm not going to even tell you, because it's embarrassing how small he is, this is The Mace!

*(**MACE.** In his mask.)*

*(Lights change. **MACE** pulls his mask up and off his face, and directly addresses the audience.)*

MACE. So every time I'm about to get in the ring, I think back to nineteen eighty-six. I'm six years old, my younger brother's five, my older brother's eight, we're sitting on cold hardwood floors on Cruger Avenue in the Bronx on Saturday mornings, eating Frosted Flakes that are really just generic flakes of corn with generic spoons of sugar sprinkled on top with a little drop of milk to give the impression that shit is gonna get soggy when even then we all know that there ain't no Tony the fucking Tiger grrrrrr-owling at our poor Puerto Rican asses from the front of that box. But still, we ate it. And we drank a quarter water right along with it. No soda in our house. Unhealthy.

So Saturday morning, on the floor, Underoos, 11am – nah. Go back to 10:45. Still on the floor, still cereal, still Underoos and shirtless, me, my brother, and my brother, and we're playing with wrestling guys. Not action figures, not dolls, nah – we played with wrestling guys. My brother and my brother, they played with the big World Wrestling Federation wrestling guys, with the big molded rubber that was like almost a foot tall and they were heavy and you couldn't even move their arms cause they came already shaped into some muscle pose – man, that shit wasn't even worth playing with. I think my brother and my brother only got them cause they looked just like the guys – I mean, the British Bulldogs, Kamala, whatever – they got the characters right, but you couldn't *wrestle* with them.

So my brother and my brother played with the big doofy WWF guys, and nah, they're not even playing with them, cause you *can't* play with them, cause they're not built to be played with really, they're built to be put on a shelf, they're not toys, but it's worse than not being toys – they're nothing, they're not *productive*, and they give you the wrong idea about what wrestling is. Those big rubber things that don't move, they make you think that wrestling is about big and static and pre-posed and color, that it's about what the toymakers dictated based on what they thought would be interesting to kids, but nah – I *was* a kid, and what was interesting to me, as a kid, was being able to do some, you know, *playing* with my fucking toys.

So what I had, I had the AWA – American Wrestling Association – wrestling guys, see, cause they were smaller, and their arms moved, and their legs moved, and the heads could even turn a little, and you could play with them, you could kind of almost have real matches and do real moves with them, but see, the thing was, nobody in New York City knew nothing about the AWA. The WWF was on TV at eleven o'clock, they had Wrestlemania, they had Cyndi Lauper and the MTV hook-up, the Rock 'n Wrestling Connection or whatever, and all that made it *look* like their toys would be fun. But those toys weren't shit. I fucking hate those toys.

MACE. *(cont.)* But the AWA guys, yo. I could tell stories with those guys. I had whole drawn out epic storylines about who hated who and who won what belt, and I acted them out with six little AWA wrestling guys. And my brothers made fun of me, and fuck them, because when the wrestling came on at 11am on Saturday morning, and they got all excited about the colors, and the music, and the like, cool, I don't know, hair or whatever the fuck they got excited about, and they would stop eating the fake Frosted Flakes and start hitting each other and trying to do the moves they saw Junkyard Dog or Ricky Steamboat or The Hart Foundation doing, while they were doing all that, I was *watching*, for real, and I was understanding every second of the stories that were being told.

So it's 11am, Saturday morning, Underoos, fake flakes, big rubber wrestling guys, small perfect wrestling guys, my brother clotheslining my brother and my brother setting my brother up to try to body slam him – and that's when my grandpa would walk in, already dressed, always dressed, the head flick up so he's looking down his nose at my brother and my brother and they stop in a second and he doesn't have to say nothing cause the bodyslamming ain't gonna happen when he's in the room, and the cup of coffee, and he looks at the TV, and he laughs, and he says:

"It takes most people a long time to know what they love in life, Grandson. But I think you already know."

(silence)

And he was right.

(MACE *remembers his grandfather. He gets lost in the memory.)*

Sorry – I get distracted sometimes. That's not even the point of the story.

So.

I got a job doing exactly what I love.

Which meant I came to work for Everett K. Olson.

(Reveal EKO.*)*

EKO. Founder, CEO, and chief creative mind behind THE largest wrestling organization in the world. The best wrestling there is, the best wrestling there was, the best wrestling there will ever be. THE wrestling.

MACE. Everett K. Olson, or as we call him, EKO, subscribes to the big, colorful, pre-posed school of running a wrestling company. Wrestling guys that look good, not wrestling guys you can play with.

EKO. What do I care if they play with our toys? I just care that they buy them.

MACE. And it's hard to argue with his results. He runs Monday night's highest ranked cable television program. He produces twelve pay-per-view broadcasts a year, each garnering nearly one million buys.

EKO. And I've made two appearances on *Dancing with the Stars.*

MACE. And he won both times. So while I vehemently and respectfully object to my boss's overly simplistic approach to my art form, I don't mention my objection. I mean, even if I did, he'd tell me –

EKO. You've got nothing to complain about, Mace. You've achieved the American Dream. You're one of THE Wrestlers.

(And EKO *is gone.)*

MACE. And he's right. I am one of THE Wrestlers. I'm one of the really fucking good THE Wrestlers, and that means, unlike other jobs where when you get really good, you become a boss or a star or you get paid more, in wrestling being really fucking good – like really fucking better than like how good you think I'm gonna be from me telling you that I'm really fucking good – when you get really good at the wrestling part of the wrestling business, you're not rewarded. You're unrewarded. De-rewarded. De-warded?

Sorry. Being really good at the wrestling part of the wrestling business means you make the other guy in the ring with you look better than he is, so you get in the ring with some guy who sucks, and he looks like he's kicking your ass, and the audience wants to see guys who can kick guys' asses, so that guy gets the applause, and then that guy gets the credit, and then the boss loves the job you did making that guy look like he didn't suck, so you get to make the next guy who sucks look like he doesn't suck, because the more guys who don't suck the better for THE Wrestling because guys who don't suck sell T-shirts, but the problem with that is that while your getting your ass kicked by guys who only look like they don't suck because you're making them look like they don't suck, the audience starts to think – guess what? *You're* the one who sucks. So then – and let's drop the metaphor cause I'm not really talking about you, but thank you for playing along – so then I go to the bottom in the minds of the boss because I'm losing so much, and as bad as I want to walk in to his corporate nightmare office and remind him that wrestling is *not a legitimate sporting event* and I am losing because *he is writing scripts that tell me to lose*, as bad as I want to tell my boss that, I don't tell him nothing.

Because it's actually a good job.

A dream job.

An Underoos-and-bootleg-Frosted-Flakes-on-the-floor daydream job.

And I'm happy to lose.

And I'm happy for the audience to tell me that I suck.

Because when I wake up in the morning, I don't even need an alarm clock.

And I don't mind that my knees hurt.

My hands hurt.

My everythings hurt.

I don't mind.

Because I'm one of THE Wrestlers.

And I'm in love with who I am.

(beat)

MACE. *(cont.)* Now I don't have no illusions about who I am though.

I am one of THE Wrestlers.

I am A THE Wrestler.

I am not THE THE Wrestler.

That's this guy.

(Music: something very hip-hop, very flashy, and somehow money-oriented. Something current and contemporary and big and obnoxious and ridiculous.)

(And that's the perfect definition of this entire section: The Elaborate Entrance of Chad Deity. It's hip-hop, it's flashy, and it's all about money.)

EKO. *(as Ring Announcer)* Ladies and Gentlemen…allow me to introduce to you…standing in at THE ideal height… weighing in at THE ideal weight…hailing from THE United States of America…he…is…THE Wrestling Champion…he…is…CHAAAAD DEEEEEITYYYYYY!

(Finally, he is revealed: **CHAD DEITY**. *He is huge. He is strong. He is extremely well-dressed. He wears a big gold championship belt. He is literally tossing money around as he enters through the audience and heads to the stage/ ring.)*

MACE. Here are the facts about Chad Deity, organized in handy numbered outline form. Number one: Chad Deity is extremely muscular.

(CHAD DEITY *strikes a pose.)*

Number two: Chad Deity has a winning smile.

(CHAD DEITY *smiles winningly.)*

Number three: Chad Deity is good on the mic.

(CHAD DEITY *is handed a microphone.)*

CHAD DEITY. Chad Deity was hanging out with his boy Derek Jeter the other day and Chad Deity's boy Derek Jeter turned to Chad Deity and said, "Chad Deity, you're the champion and the ladies' man and the media icon that I've always wanted to be," and Chad Deity looked at his boy Derek Jeter and said… "Chad Deity knows, Derek Jeter. Chad Deity knows."

MACE. Number four: Chad Deity has made a lot of money for THE Wrestling, thanks to numbers one through three.

CHAD DEITY. Number four A: Chad Deity has made a lot of money for Chad Deity, thanks to number four.

MACE. Number four A one: Macedonio Guerra has not made himself even a fraction of what Chad Deity has made, even though you could argue that the Macedonio Guerras of the wrestling world are just as essential to the success of THE Wrestling as the Chad Deities –

CHAD DEITY. There ain't Chad Deities.

MACE. – The one, the only, THE Chad Deity. And the reason why I am as important to his success – which means the success of THE Wrestling – the reason why I am as important to the myth of Chad Deity as Chad Deity himself is fact number five:

CHAD DEITY. Chad Deity is a terrible wrestler.

MACE. He's got charisma.

CHAD DEITY. Charisma owes Chad money.

MACE. He's got the look.

(**CHAD DEITY** *rips off his shirt and poses.*)

He's not above cheesy shit like that.

CHAD DEITY. Not even remotely above it!

MACE. He's got everything you need to be a superstar wrestler. Cause remember, being talented really ain't a factor of key importance.

CHAD DEITY. Not even remotely important!

MACE. When I'm on the attack in a wrestling match, it's a constant process of action, reaction, and evaluation, thinking about the outcome of the match, which yes, we already know going into the night, so don't dismiss my art form on the basis of it being predetermined unless you're ready to dismiss ballet for the swan already knowing it's gonna end up dead. I'm listening to the crowd and assessing how much they hate me, deciding whether my next move should be high-flying and fancy or evil and nefarious, figuring out at every step of the process exactly how best to tell our story – and I'm the guy who they all think sucks, because when Chad Deity is on the attack, his thought process is a little more easy to follow:

CHAD DEITY. Punch! Punch! Clothesline! Elbow Drop! Pick 'em up – Powerbomb 'em – Pin 'em.

MACE. That's the most popular wrestler in THE Wrestling, folks.

CHAD DEITY. Mace, come here and let me powerbomb you, brother.

MACE. No offense to you all, but I only take powerbombs when I'm getting paid. Let's go to the videotape.

(**MACE** *shows video of* **CHAD DEITY** *powerbombing him.*)

You see, when Chad Deity powerbombs me – and it's happened a lot over the years – I allow myself to be bent over with my head between his legs.

I jump into the air when he's pretending to pick me up.

I bend my body in half and sit straight up and elevate myself into position on his shoulders.

CHAD DEITY. Then Chad Deity takes over.

MACE. He falls forward.

CHAD DEITY. That's my part.

MACE. He doesn't even do that so good. I smack both hands on the mat to evenly distribute the impact throughout my back.

I keep my chin tucked into my chest to prevent concussions.

And most important to the reputation of the champion of THE Wrestling –

CHAD DEITY. – Chad Deity –

MACE. – I bounce off the mat and convulse in pain and scream and howl to make it seem like this guy, this unbelievably untalented freak of physical and charismatic nature is actually worth a damn as a professional wrestler.

CHAD DEITY. Teamwork.

MACE. It is teamwork, even if I'm the only one on the team doing the work. And that, ladies and gentlemen, not the storylines, not the competition, not the dazzling physiques or the pretty colors or the elaborate entrance of Chad Deity is the reason that professional wrestling is the most uniquely profound artistic expression of the ideals of the United States:

CHAD DEITY. In wrestling, you can't kick a guy's ass without the help of the guy whose ass you're kicking.

MACE. People love the powerbomb. They love the power, the beauty, the implausibility of it. People know that the powerbomb requires me and The Champ to unite to make it look like he's murdering me, when in actuality I'm doing what I can to make him look like the all-world fighting machine he's made out to be, and he's doing what he can with his limited capacity to make sure I don't break my neck, and so at the bottom of what we're doing is we're both trying to ensure that neither one of us gets hurt. That fact is powerful and beautiful and, like I said, one of the most profound expressions of the ideals of this nation.

CHAD DEITY. Pick 'em up – Powerbomb 'em – Pin 'em.

(**EKO** *appears.*)

EKO. We should put that on a T-shirt.

(*into Bluetooth*)

Did you hear that? Have those ready by intermission.

MACE. And that right there – the catchphrases, the T-shirts – that's why Chad Deity is more important to Everett K. Olson than Macedonio Guerra is.

EKO. That's not your name.

MACE. In THE Wrestling, I'm known as The Mace.

EKO. That other name is too hard to pronounce.

MACE. For white people.

CHAD DEITY. I can't pronounce it.

MACE. For non-Spanish speaking Americans.

EKO. For wrestling fans. Wrestling fans do not speak Spanish.

MACE. He's my boss, so I don't bring up Lucha Libre, or the World Wrestling Council in Puerto Rico, or the late Eddie Guerrero or Carlos Colon or El Hijo Del Santo or…I don't bring up any of them. I let my boss be right.

EKO. Now put on your mask. Time for the show.

(EKO and CHAD exit.)

MACE. I don't bring up how the mask is a sanctified, holy Mexican wrestling tradition. I know my role. I shut my mouth. I know that tonight, The Mace will go out there and put on a show and Chad Deity will be the benefactee of all my hard work. I know that even if I'm the AWA wrestling guy, and I have multiple points of articulation, which is what they call the movable parts these days, and you can use me to tell a real story, and even if Chad Deity is the big, unbendable, pre-posed lump of hockey puck rubber that ain't really good for nothing but collecting dust on a back shelf, I know my brother and my brother would still rather play with Chad Deity, and the rest of the United States would still rather play with Chad Deity, and ultimately, because of that undeniable fact, I know that Chad Deity deserves every ounce of respect and dollars and championship gold that he receives. And I know that the only role that I'm destined to fulfill in all my days in THE Wrestling, as long as they may last, is the one I'm in right now: Jobber to the Stars. The guy who loses to make the winners look good.

(silence)

MACE. *(cont.)* Whatever. None of this is the point of the story either.

So my brother and my brother – remember them? – they moved to Red Hook, Brooklyn. And every weekend they cross the Brooklyn Queens Expressway into Carroll Gardens to play basketball, cause they're so fucking predictable and they gotta go play basketball like every other kid in our Like-Mike-If-I-Could-Be-Like-Mike generation. And whenever they're playing basketball in Carroll Gardens, they call to tell me about this kid.

(VIGNESHWAR PADUAR (VP), on a cell phone.)

VP. Nah, but –

MACE. This tall, lanky, Indian kid.

VP. Nah, but –

MACE. He calls himself VP.

VP. Nah, but baby, mira, I'm saying, but –
I'm saying! Carajo, I'm saying –
Cause I'm Indian. Cause I'm fucking Indian.
Nah, but that's my culture, Baby. You don't know nothing about my culture. You're Dominican.
Nah, I'm not saying Dominicans are stupid.
I'm saying, you Dominican, so you ain't never had no reason to know nothing about no Indians.
Until me.

MACE. My brother and my brother find the kid's use of Spanish slang when he's hitting on Latinas hilarious, and since the kid stays steady hitting on Latinas – and well, women in general – my brother and my brother stay calling me. And once in a while if I get lucky, I get to hear when he stops hitting on Latinas – or well, women in general – cause when he stops hitting on them, most of the time it gets funnier.

(VP, covering the phone as he yells to someone offstage.)

VP. Motherfucker, you step on my sneakers again and I will fuck your ass up.

Me and my whole country got the capabilities.

Long-range nuclear missile status, doggy.

We the new Superpower.

We make your Jordans, train your doctors, AND help desk your ass when your Mac breaks down.

New Superpower, suckas. Get your ass up off my street with that shit.

(back to the phone)

Nah, pero Mamita, oye what I'm saying about India: Kama. Sutra.

MACE. And then, my brother and my brother hang up the phone, cause VP is ready to get game. And I sit in my hotel room, moderately obsessed with the way this kid works with words, switches codes, drops slang and makes me laugh, indirect, him in his cell phone and me on my brother's or my brother's. And a few hours later, my brother and my brother call me, and they tell me the same thing every time: VP wrecked us on the court, they say.

This kid, he can play they say.

Like Billy Hoyle in *White Men Can't Jump*, like he's hustling us, yo.

Like he comes in, goofy, awkward, Indian, man.

Not even Chinese, so you get a little of that Yao Ming warning shot.

He's INDIAN.

And he speaks Spanish.

Fuck that, he could trash talk you in English, Spanish, Hindi, and Urdu and I stay listening cause I didn't even know my brother knew that Urdu was a word, let alone a language. And I realize that it's changing the entire way they look at the world to find this Indian, this Indian, I don't know, this Indian fucking rock star. And then one time, my brother and my brother say: I'd pay to see this kid.

(beat)

MACE. *(cont.)* I'd *pay* to see this kid.

(beat)

They see him every week, and they'd pay to see this kid.

(beat)

Now THIS is the point of the story.

Next time THE Wrestling comes to New York to do a show, I head straight down to Carroll Gardens, in theory to play basketball with my brother and my brother, but really to watch basketball, but really to watch my brother and my brother and really really, to watch VP, who is really Vigneshwar Paduar.

VP. The mayor of Smith Street.

MACE. Smith Street is the hopping new social center of Brooklyn reborn.

VP. BROOKLYN, WHAT!

MACE. Vigneshwar Paduar's family owns a gas station by the F train at Carroll Street, a pizzeria near Bergen, a botanica one block in from Atlantic Avenue, and an apartment building just off the BQE.

VP. LUXURY LOFTS, WHAT!

MACE. Everything my brother and my brother said about this kid was true and insufficient. His mouth never stops moving. Trash talk in English, Spanish, Hindi, and Urdu, yes, but sprinklings of Polish, Italian – shit, when a Japanese girl strolls past:

VP. *(in Japanese)* Yaa, yaa, kawaiko-chan. Ocha demo shinai? *(Hey, hey, cutie. Can I take you out for tea?)*

MACE. And he gets the number. And he wins the game. And I end up amazed. And I end up talking to him.

(to **VP***)*

You ever think about going pro?

VP. Man, basketball ain't no kind of job. I'm an entertainer, Papa. All I need is an audience and there's audience everywhere.

MACE. I think that's about that – he already is where he really wants to be, because anywhere he goes, he is the party, he is the most amazing thing happening in the room. And then he says something, the thing, the one sentence that impacts the rest of my life more than anything I heard before:

VP. Nah, I need more than an audience.

MACE. You do?

VP. I need, what I need is, I need that Larry Bird vs. Magic Johnson, that rivalry, only I don't care about trying to beat him and winning some fucking championship ring –

MACE. – that shit's going on your finger for a minute then off to eBay anyway –

VP. – I want to be working with somebody, I want him to elevate me –

MACE. – to push you, to make you work harder –

VP. – and have my back –

MACE. – and make sure he don't hurt you –

VP. – and it ain't nothing that's romantic or love or nothing like that –

MACE. It's community.

VP. It's fucking community.

(*silence*)

MACE. I'm gonna get you a job.

(**VP** *exits.*)

MACE. (*cont.*) Now it's not my place to get involved in the money side of THE Wrestling. I ain't a financial factor far as EKO is concerned, and I ain't ultimately interested in making no more money for no one and I don't need no more money for me since I came from watered-down sugar flakes and sugar water and I figure anything I got that ain't got water and sugar in the name is gravy, so I stick on out of business discussions. But VP knows what I know, what any professional wrestler who really understands what he does for a living knows, which is that the value of two men in silly outfits pretending to beat each other into submission is not in the fight – it's in the communion. And those are just his intangibles. With the tangibles this kid brings to the table, he could outshine even the elaborate entrance of Chad Deity.

(Music: It's hip-hop and it's impossible not to dance to it and oh man, what a party.)

(It's the soundtrack for this little section: call it The Elaborate Entrance of Vigneshwar Paduar.)

EKO. *(as Ring Announcer)* Ladies and Gentlemen, the following contest is scheduled for one fall, with a next generation of human history time limit.

(This is Chad Deity's Elaborate Entrance but bigger and more exciting.)

Introducing first, hailing from Mumbai Do-Or-Die, India; hailing from the planet of Brooklyn, New York; hailing from the new global society; weighing in at an incalculable sociopolitical weight; he is the future of professional wrestling; fuck that, he is the future of the world; he is VIGNESHWAR PADUAR!

(The Elaborate Entrance of Vigneshwar Paduar needs to convince the audience that he is a can't miss star.)

(And at the end, reveal Everett K. Olson watching the whole thing.)

EKO. I don't think there's a place in the company for him.

(Everything involved in the entrance disappears, leaving only EKO, MACE, and VP.)

MACE. I suggest I'd take a pay cut.

EKO. I don't pay you enough to split your salary.

MACE. I suggest maybe Chad Deity doesn't need quite so elaborate an entrance.

(silence)

EKO. Mace, Mace, Mace.

I'm going to pretend you didn't say that.

Let me explain this to you again.

MACE. He explains this to me a lot.

EKO. Chad Deity's elaborate entrance makes soldiers remember what they fight for, makes fathers teach their sons to stand up and cheer on greatness. Chad Deity's elaborate entrance, by proxy, is America's elaborate entrance, ongoing, giving proof through the night that the flag is still there. Chad Deity's elaborate entrance defeats demons, and we feel like our demons deserve that defeat, and we feel, more importantly, that we can be the ones to defeat them.

MACE. My boss has a knack for overstating his case. He's also got an uncanny understanding of the THE Wrestling audience and exactly what they want to see. And when he mentions the demons, he looks to VP, and he looks to me...and he seems to have an idea.

EKO. Your boy, this, this kid, this – where is he from anyway?

MACE. Brooklyn.

EKO. No, I mean, he's brown, not like you, and that's not racist, so relax.

What is he, Afghan? Oriental?

MACE. That's a rug. And a rug. But I don't tell my boss that. I tell him Vigneshwar Paduar is from India.

EKO. He's not a fundamentalist, is he? I think I might be able to sell a fundamentalist.

MACE. I don't mention that the history of professional wrestling is filled with sloppy generic Middle East stereotypes and Russian stereotypes and Native American stereotypes and *Samoan* stereotypes and it's bullshit and it's bullshit...but I don't mention it. Instead VP and I propose a little outer borough counter-action.

(VP enters.)

VP. Call my character the Son of Shiva, Hindu god of Death and Destruction. I'll break my opponents' bodies, shatter their souls – and then tell them it's all for their higher consciousness, some hippie bullshit –

MACE. He wasn't feeling that.

VP. Aight, fuck that – we don't play up India. We go to Brooklyn. Viggie Smalls is the illest. The Notorious V.I.G. The Leader of the V-V-V-V-V-V-V-Unit.

(rapping)

So dope in the ring that it's really unfair

I see your boys in the back and I'm killing 'em there

Now ladies don't worry it ain't silly to stare

You getting pinned by the slumdog milli-a-naire

MACE. It's an unlikely thing to see, this kid with the brown skin that's not brown like my brown which ain't brown like the brown that folks like my boss expect to hear words like this flowing out of, and that's why it's money.

VP. It worked for John Cena, and he's a white kid from Boston – from BOSTON! You got me, from the home of hip-hop –

MACE. – I don't stop him to say that Brooklyn ain't the home of hip-hop, even though as a Bronx kid, I'm deeply offended –

VP. You got me, VP, and I can make this work like no one else, see?

MACE. And EKO looks up from his computer screen and gives the dismissive hand wave I-ain't-feeling-it kind of move.

EKO. What kind of street credibility can I sell between the coasts with a skinny paki?

MACE. I cringe, but VP doesn't even slow down to acknowledge that (a) he ain't from Pakistan and therefore (b) he ain't a paki, and (c) how the fuck you gonna call someone a paki in the first place? And for a second I think about Everett K. Olson complaining about the spic he's got curtain jerking under some stupid mask, or the nigger his company is built around. Nah – he'd never call Chad Deity a nigger. Chad Deity is no nigger to Everett K. Olson. Chad Deity is a money machine. The spic and the paki haven't made EKO a dime.

VP. That's cool – the Brooklyn thing don't take advantage of the fact that me and my people are the new superpower anyway. You know we're the new superpower, right? Brazil and Russia and India and China – that's the BRIC. And yo, I speak all kinds of Indian and some kinds of Chinese and the Brazilian's just like Spanish and give me a week in Brighton Beach, I'll pick up the Russian. I'll pick up a bunch of Russians.

MACE. And I look at the boss, and I can see he wants to wave this off, but VP's in his element now, and when this kid's in motion like this, ain't nobody interested in stopping him.

VP. So you put me in a suit, and I'm talking about outsourcing tech jobs and I'm talking about our ever-growing economic and cultural cpaital while the American economy is melting right before their eyes. And I'll do it in six different languages. They'll hate me.

MACE. I think this one has a chance, seeing as how it stirs up the kind of nationalistic fear and loathing for an exotic outsider that this industry loves and has thrived on, and Everett K. Olson is actually listening and he's thinking hard and –

EKO. THAT'S IT!

MACE. That's it?

VP. Fuck right, that's it.

EKO. What wrestling needs right now is a Muslim fundamentalist!

MACE. Fuck. There's already been a Muslim fundamentalist in professional wrestling. Muhammad Hassan. It didn't end well. Google it. I don't mention this.

EKO. Only problem is, I don't know what we got with this kid.

MACE. He's got a point. VP isn't a wrestler. I hadn't really thought about that until right now.

EKO. But we make him a fundamentalist, we say he's from someplace else –

(into Bluetooth)

Where are Muslims from? A cave, right?

(to MACE)

A fucking cave or something, and we put somebody else with him to handle the heavy lifting.

MACE. And as soon as my boss mentions the heavy lifting, everything comes clear and I understand why I was the one who had a brother and a brother who crossed the BQE to find this kid – I'm his heavy lifting. Charisma-challeneged wrestlers like me have always been paired with smooth talkers like VP. He can be my manager, trash-talking our enemies, bragging and boasting and making everyone want to see us get beat, and then I can get in the ring and back up every inch of that talk with the best wrestling performance this company has ever seen. Just like I always dreamed. And I'll never have to worry about saying a word.

(to EKO)

I'll do the heavy lifting.

EKO. You? You're gonna talk for him?

(silence)

MACE. Um. Everett K. Olson wants someone to *talk* for Vigneshwar Paduar?

EKO. The kid is supposed to be this militant cave-dwelling fuck-damentalist, right? And he's in here rapping and sounding like your average street hood from cell block C.

MACE. Everett K. Olson wants someone to *talk* for *Vigneshwar Paduar.*

EKO. We need someone…someone to manage him. Someone to come out and speak Arabic and rant and rave and really give the suckers in the cheap seats something to get riled up over.

MACE. Go home and Google Muhammad Hassan tonight. Please.

EKO. And what am I gonna do, send him out there with some Cuban kid –

MACE. – Puerto Rican –

EKO. – to rant and rave in Spanish –

MACE. Spanglish. At best.

EKO. And piss off the crowd for this Israeli Iraqi whatever he is?

MACE. Israeli? I can't even.

EKO. Mace, Mace, Mace – you don't work for this, Mace.

(**CHAD DEITY** *is revealed somewhere in the room – he's been there the whole time, unnoticed. Maybe he's in an oversized chair facing away and spins into view.*)

CHAD DEITY. Make him Mexican.

VP. The fuck did he come from?

CHAD DEITY. Mexican guy, hates America, hates freedom, comes here to steal away jobs, leech off services, make our good hard-earned American money and send it back to his little militant revolutionary comrades in Mexico. And he's got connections with Iran for the nukes and Kenya for the – what does Kenya have?

EKO. Socialism!

CHAD DEITY. – and those all connect him with Al-Qaeda and Hamas and the French for the destruction of the greatest country on Earth. And the Mexican enlists this great Origami warrior, trained in the deadly MMA – Muslim Martial Arts – where they believe you can murder a man with pressure points and prayer.

EKO. You gotta admit, the kid has that look.

CHAD DEITY. And the Mexican and the Middle Easterner come to the States and they want to bring us down from the inside –

EKO. So they figure the best way to do that is to start at the top with a major symbolic victory –

CHAD DEITY. So they come to THE Wrestling –

EKO. They come after Chad Deity –

CHAD DEITY. They come after the heart of America.

MACE. I definitely don't tell them that there is no country named America.

EKO. Mace, Mace, Mace, this could work, Mace.

MACE. This isn't what we're –

VP. Let's do it.

> *(pause)*

> Yeah. We're in. Let's do it.

MACE. And I look over at Vigneshwar Paduar, and he doesn't say anything else, and he doesn't have to say anything else, because it's instantly clear that he's not unfamiliar with anything that's happening right now. He's heard it on basketball courts and in pizza places and from beautiful but ignorant Brooklynites with words like "pink" and "hottie" stenciled across subtle sagged sweatpants. He's heard this. He's fought it. He's beaten it not through fistfights and the stink of swagger, but through no look passes and perfect pepperoni slices and multiple ripple-effect orgasms. I look to VP and he tells me without speaking, he tells me that the best way he knows to overcome is by taking up the challenge and ripping the terms of that challenge to his own, new, fashionable shreds.

VP. We'll do it.

MACE. So we did it.

> *(**EKO, VP,** and **CHAD DEITY** exit.)*

> The first thing Everett K. Olson did with his newly created Axis of Enemy Combatants was to script our debut promo – the moment that The Fundamentalist – yeah, that's the name he came up with – and Che Chavez Castro – I swear, folks, this is what I'm working against here – the moment that The Fundamentalist and Che Chavez Castro were first unveiled to a national television audience. The second thing Everett K. Olson did was to disavow any association with the words we were about to speak.

(**EKO**, *addressing the television audience.*)

EKO. The views and opinions expressed in the following do not represent the views of THE Wrestling. In fact, on behalf of THE Wrestling, I would like to condemn the comments to which you are, unfortunately, about to be subjected.

MACE. I don't mention that it's his fault that people are about to be subjected to our comments…or that he wrote our comments. Instead, as usual, I go ahead and do what I have been paid to do.

(**VP** *enters as The Fundamentalist.* **VP** *prays.*)

(**MACE** *changes to his Che Chavez Castro costume. He speaks with an exaggerated Mexican accent and delivers a bad, over-the-top wrestling promo.*)

MACE. *(as Che Chavez Castro)* Attention Capitalist pigs! I am Che Chavez Castro, Mexican revolutionary and denouncer of all things American!

I have traveled long y far in search for freedom, in search for a better life, in search for…America. And now I have crossed the border. I have found riches and happiness and the American Dream…and I hate it.

VP. From the audience, silence.

I'm gonna jump in for my boy while he's in character, if that's cool. Thanks.

They want to boo us. They want to do exactly what Everett K. Olson expects them to want to do, which is wrap themselves in an American flag and tell us to go back where we came from, tell us to love it or leave it, tell us U-S-A, U-S-A and everything that goes along with jingo patriot mindless entertainment national empowerment via men playfighting in spandex panties. But they can't. The words coming out of Mace's mouth don't let them. The words are foolish. The audience has heard them before. We're a caricature in a world of cartoons. We're pencil sketched. The audience wants animation and color.

MACE. I am consumed with hatred of everything that your nation stands for, and as a Mexican man of action, I have decided to take a stand.

VP. And that's my cue. And I nail it. I rise from prayer, Muslim prayer I assume, although I'm not sure my turban and my Greek worry beads and my yoga mat are exactly Allah-approved. I pose fear-inspiringly. I glare. I lock my eyes on the camera, and I glare, and I got no expression on my face, and Mace vibes off it, he feels it, and his voice settles in, and he's getting creepy, and it's powerful, and it's a start.

MACE. And this is the stand I have chosen to take. Behold The Fundamentalist.

VP. And some music starts, and I think it's a Bollywood love song, but it might be cut with some chanting Tibetan monks and maybe I even hear some Riverdance Gaelic shit someplace in the mix. But me and Mace, we keep glaring, and we ain't speaking, and the pose we hit and the look we give and the connection me and him got on some psychic mind meld status, like those evil twin brothers from G.I. Joe, all that combines to make the nonsense fade to the background just long enough that we feel like we did everything that could be done with what they gave us. And we don't say another word.

MACE. *(as himself)* We stare them the fuck down.

VP. And it's silent. And they're scared.

MACE. And it's way better than anyone could have expected.

(EKO *'s office*)

EKO. Guys, guys, this is great. Don't change a thing. Don't change a thing. Less words, maybe. The silent part, that's gold. Less words. They'll hate you.

(EKO *exits.*)

MACE. They'll hate us. In this business, that's about the best thing you can hear. And it took me I don't know how many years, and I had to do it as Che Chavez Castro, the Mexican revolutionary and generic Middle East sympathizer, and I don't know for exact what I did, but tonight, I did something, and it was something good, and it was alongside someone who I trust, and all I know is we're gonna build on that, and all I know is somehow I've been building on that since cold hardwood Saturday mornings in 1986. We took the wrong thing. We made it the right thing. I'm proud of that. So next week…we go ahead and do it again.

(**EKO**, *addressing the television audience.*)

EKO. The views and opinions expressed in the following do not represent the views of THE Wrestling. In fact, on behalf of THE Wrestling, I would like to condemn the comments to which you are, unfortunately, about to be subjected.

VP. Only we don't make no comments. We make shit uncomfortable and creepy.

Thirty seconds they give us onscreen.

MACE. Thirty seconds we don't speak.

VP. We ain't saying shit.

MACE. And neither is the audience. Ten seconds we stare at the camera. Intensity.

VP. And I catch the ghost or something – I rip off the prayer robe shawl tent thing they have me in this week, and I throw it on the floor and I throw myself on the floor and I start doing one-handed push-ups and yo, I never knew I could do one-handed push-ups but I bang them the fuck out and I keep my eyes on the camera the whole time.

MACE. And I stay where I am in the back of the frame and I glare.

VP. And fifteen seconds after the push-ups start, I'm back on my feet, and I'm sweating just a little, and I got perfect drops, two of them, dripping slow and tracing the bends of the bones in my face, and I'm right back where I came from, me and Macedonio Guerra – fuck that Chavez Castro shit – me and my boy Mace scaring the back of the neck of every wrestling fan in the country.

MACE. And in the last two seconds, it feels so much like the moment when you realize who you are and what you do and why you do and where you fit that a smile breaks in the back corner of the left side of my mouth.

VP. At the same time the same smile breaks on mine. Perfect.

(EKO's office)

EKO. Chill bumps you guys are giving me. Back of my leg, every hair is running away from every other hair.

MACE. Generally nothing Everett K. Olson says by way of praise means a thing. Still this feels pretty fucking good.

EKO. And I think the excitement has left the front of my boxer briefs a little wet.

VP. Dude.

EKO. They don't know what to make of you two. They know they want to boo you and they know they will boo you but right now they don't know where you're coming from and it scares the fucking fuck out of their fucking fuck fucks.

I might never have the neither of you speak again.

(into Bluetooth)

Order me new underwear!

*(**CHAD DEITY** is revealed somewhere in the room with a loaf of raisin bread.)*

CHAD DEITY. The government demands that there be a minimum number of raisins in raisin bread.

*(all eyes on **CHAD DEITY**)*

It's true. Says so right here on the back of The Champ's bag of raisin bread.

VP. You know, we're actually in the middle of something –

CHAD DEITY. Don't worry – you're not bothering The Champ.

You see, brother, most people find the government's involvement in raisin bread allotment kind of ridiculous. But not Chad Deity, no way, baby. Chad Deity knows that it is *not* ridiculous. Chad Deity knows that this is the United States of America! This is the greatest country in the world! We deserve the best: the best economy, the best armed forces, the best wrestling champion. And god damn it, we deserve the best and biggest and most raisins in each and every bite of every slice of every loaf of our raisin bread. That, my friends, is the American Dream. That, my friends, is what Chad Deity stands for, and The Champ, for one, is glad that the US Government sees things his way.

And you, Mace, of all the people in this room, should understand the American Dream, particularly as relates to raisin bread, because your people fought, and protested, and boycotted for the right to pick grapes.

MACE. I'm not Mexican.

CHAD DEITY. This no word thing you're doing? The Champ approves. Not a bad start.

VP. Not a bad start? The audience is eating it up.

CHAD DEITY. Sure. For now. But sooner or later, they're going to want you to speak.

What are you going to have to say?

(silence)

You ain't got the raisins, brother. Right now, you're giving them bread, and it's different bread, so they're excited while they figure out what to do with it. But eventually they're gonna realize you don't work for French toast, they're gonna realize you don't work for cream cheese and jelly, and they'll come looking for the raisins.

(CHAD DEITY exits.)

EKO. He's right, you know.

You're doing good. You're doing fine. But we could use…we could use some more words. That's the reason we've got you in there with him, Mace. You're the one who I'm paying to deliver the raisins.

(EKO exits.)

MACE. I'm accustomed to this kind of Chad-inspired change of mind from the boss so it's easy for me to keep my mouth shut and let it slide. But VP? Not so much.

VP. I might never have the neither of you speak again. Chill bumps you guys are giving me. The front of my boxer briefs –

MACE. – Dude.

VP. Ay yo, get both those dudes back in here and let's get this all understood that we don't need to hear what they think they know about what you and me are doing out there.

MACE. I let VP vent –

VP. – Pepperidge Farm ass motherfuckers.

MACE. – and when he's good and vented, I let him know that I spent the whole raisin conversation thinking about what we were gonna do next week. I spent the whole raisin conversation thinking about the only two words we possibly needed to say.

(**EKO**, *addressing the television audience.*)

EKO. The views and opinions expressed in the following do not represent the views of THE Wrestling. In fact, on behalf of THE Wrestling, I would like to condemn the comments to which you are, unfortunately, about to be subjected.

VP. First thing you see after Everett K. Olson disavows all connection with everything you're about to see is –

(**VP** *holds up a life-size poster of* **CHAD DEITY**.)

MACE. *(matter-of-fact)* Chad Deity.

VP. Every five, six seconds or so, Mace drops that name, and every time he spits that name, the name of the champion of the world, all I do is smirk.

MACE. *(mocking)* Chad Deity.

VP. Every time that name shoots out of Mace's mouth, my mind races to raisin bread, and that takes care of the smirk – couldn't hold my ridicule in if I tried. And I got exactly zero interest in trying.

MACE. *(angry)* Chad Deity.

VP. We got a Black world champion and he's rich and he God Blesses America, and he talks vociferous and he's non-threatening unless you yourself are a threat to that which he God Blesses, and you ain't a threat because you're physically imposing or because you might pull off your fucking dashiki – or whatever the fuck you terrorist types wear – and bomb an arena full of God-fearing, Chad Deity-fearing, tax-paying, ticket-buying Americans, but you're a threat because Chad Deity drew a fucking line in the sand and instead of stepping over that line so Chad Deity could pick you up, powerbomb you, pin you, you held your ground and didn't speak and dared that dude to meet you on your side of his stupid fucking line of fiction.

MACE. *(disgusted)* Chad Deity.

VP. And my Indian ass stands right here next to my Puerto Rican brother, Macedonio Guerra, and every time that name shoots out of his mouth, I can feel him drifting back to The Bronx while it was burning and being told to drop dead, drifting back to Vieques and mandated sterilization and a commonwealth government without the money to keep itself in business and illegal occupations, and extraordinary rendition, and fuck that – right now a nation full of "patriots" who love to complain about how fucked up everything is, but ain't willing to sacrifice a goddamn thing for the benefit of the greater good – and Chad Deity's still out here God Blessing America. And yeah, wrestling don't got nothing to do with politics, and Chad Deity ain't the reason that what's wrong is wrong, but for someone who represents everything that's supposed to be right, that motherfucker ain't yet gave me one reason to respect him.

MACE. *(furious)* Chad –

(VP spits in the face of the poster.)

– Deity.

(*VP exits.*)

In an argument in the streets, the crowd watching things unfold will always let you know when a nerve's been struck.

(**EKO, CHAD DEITY**, *and anyone else available from off-stage as the crowd in the streets.*)

EKO, CHAD DEITY, & ALL.
OOOOOOOOOOOOOHHHHHH SHIT.

MACE. When The Fundamentalist spits in the face of Chad Deity, twenty-five thousand people in the arena and millions watching at home go –

EKO, CHAD DEITY, & ALL.
OOOOOOOOOOOOOHHHHHH SHIT.

MACE. We only put two raisins in our bread. But they were some big fucking raisins.

End of Act One
Intermission

ACT TWO

(EKO, in the ring.)

EKO. *(as Ring Announcer)* The following contest is scheduled for one fall with a forty-five minute time limit. Introducing first to my right... The Bad Guy!

(THE BAD GUY enters, antagonizing the fans.)

And his opponent...

(The Elaborate Enterance of Chad Deity begins.)

(CHAD DEITY enters)

(The match begins. CHAD DEITY destroys THE BAD GUY. Kicks, punches, body slams – basic and angry. THE BAD GUY gets no offense in.)

(After about thirty seconds of punishment, CHAD DEITY picks THE BAD GUY up, powerbombs him, pins him.)

(EKO returns to the ring.)

The winner of this match, and STILL THE Wrestling Champion –

(CHAD DEITY snatches the microphone out of the EKO's hand.)

CHAD DEITY. Do you know how many crispers I have in my refrigerator? I have four. Four crispers. Two on the bottom, two on the top. Right where your freezer is on your refrigerator, that's where I have two extra crispers. My freezer is as big as your refrigerator, and my crispers are as big as your freezer, and I don't even use a crisper.

My son, he's got a refrigerator, a mini-refrigerator downstairs in the part of the house that's special devoted to him. You know what's in his crispers? Chad Deity action figures. He likes his toys cold. I don't know – he's a weird kid. But my son gets what he wants. Unless what he wants is wrong. And my son, he knows what's right and what's wrong. And because he knows what's right and what's wrong, my son knows not to spit in anyone's face. Ever.

And you, Mace, you might be Che Chavez Castro or whatever you're choosing to call yourself now, but a month ago you were under a mask getting picked up and powerbombed and pinned in every arena THE Wrestling traveled to. And me and EKO, we told you how you could change that, and Mace, you were making progress, but now, you mention my name, you spit in my face, and the decision's made.

Chad Deity has to answer, and you both have to go down, and go down big, and you'll both be back under masks the night after I pin The Fundamentalist and send him back to Turkmenistan or Filipinostan or Voltronistan or wherever we decide he came from.

That's what you're missing in this Macedonio. We decide. Me and EKO. We decide. You just made our decision easy and obvious. Two crispers for Vigneshwar. Two crispers for Macedonio. Four crispers for Chad Deity. Unused.

(**CHAD DEITY** *exits.*)

(**MACE** *enters.*)

MACE. Chad Deity is angry.

When Chad Deity is angry onscreen, that's good for business.

THE Wrestling makes a lot of money from Chad Deity being angry on television.

When Chad Deity is angry behind the scenes?

That's a little more complicated.

And now Chad Deity is angry at me and VP.

That's a lot more complicated.

Cause remember: in wrestling, you can't kick a guy's ass without the help of *the guy whose ass you're kicking.*

Of course, you also can't kick a guy's ass if he doesn't know how to make it look like you're kicking his ass.

(**VP** *enters*)

I still gotta teach VP to wrestle.

(**VP** *trips while entering the ring.*)

Excuse me. We've got a lot of work to do.

(**MACE** *joins* **VP** *in the ring.*)

Okay. First thing we've got to do is teach you how to take a bump. How to fall.

(*Reveal* **EKO,** *with* **THE BAD GUY.**)

EKO. Mace, Mace, Mace.

The THE Wrestling fan is not interested in guys who fall.

The THE Wrestling fan is interested in guys who *make* guys fall.

(*to* **VP**)

Kid, don't worry about the bumps.

We need to start out by picking your *finisher.*

MACE. The finisher is wrestling's version of the knockout blow. Each wrestler has a unique move they use to put his opponent away. Chad Deity's finisher is, of course, the powerbomb. Mace's finisher... well, I don't ever get to put my opponents away.

Whatever. Let's stick with The Champ.

When Chad Deity hits the powerbomb, fans know to stand, to cheer.

The night is over. The day is won. You saw what you came to see.

You go to a baseball game, and Slugger McHometeam isn't guaranteed to hit a home run that day, no matter what he's been shooting slash ingesting into his body –

THE BAD GUY. – Allegedly.

EKO. We don't know anything about those kinds of substances here in THE Wrestling.

(awkward silence)

EKO. Now, the obvious finisher for The Fundamentalist is the Camel Clutch. Show him the Camel Clutch.

(THE BAD GUY *puts* **MACE** *into the Camel Clutch.* **MACE** *screams in pain, then speaks calmly while still in the hold.)*

MACE. You know who did the Camel Clutch? The Iron Sheik. Sabu. The aforementioned Muhammad Hassan – all you with iPhones saw that when you Googled him at intermission. I'm onto you.

(THE BAD GUY *releases the hold.)*

Every wrestler who has ever been portrayed as having "Middle Eastern" ancestry has done the Camel Clutch. Because Middle Easterners ride camels. So they do the Camel Clutch. I swear to God I fucking hate wrestling sometimes. I don't mention this hatred.

(to **EKO***)*

You know what I'm thinking, Boss? I'm thinking we go in a different direction.

EKO. There is no different direction. He's a fundamentalist. The Camel Clutch is fundamental.

MACE. I fucking hate wrestling.

(to **EKO***)*

No, you're right, you're right, but I'm thinking…quick strike capability.

EKO. I'm listening.

MACE. He's a threat, right? A terrorist threat. And what's the scary thing about terrorism? It can come from anywhere at any time. You don't see it coming.

VP. It's the shadowy nature of a sleeper cell.

(beat)

What? I can bullshit too, motherfucker.

EKO. Sleeper cell? I like it.

MACE. I'm thinking the superkick, boss.

(to audience)

This is the superkick.

(**MACE** *superkicks* **THE BAD GUY**. *It's quick, it's out of nowhere, it knocks* **THE BAD GUY** *off his feet.*)

You might see a match where a wrestler gets shoved off the top rope, through a table, down to the concrete floor *directly on his head* – and he still gets up to fight. Now that same wrestler, same match, he gets hit with a superkick –

(**MACE** *superkicks* **THE BAD GUY** *again.*)

– dude could be laid out for the rest of the night. In the physics of professional wrestling, as in life, the shot that knocks you out is the one you never see coming.

EKO. I like it. Use it, kid. We need a new exotic name for it. I'm thinking…

MACE. Please don't let him say it.

EKO. I'm thinking…

MACE. He's gonna say it.

EKO. The Camel Kick?

(**VP** *goes to superkick* **EKO**.)

(**MACE** *stops him.*)

Or maybe…Koran Kick. Kabbalah Kick. I don't know. I'll figure it out. I like it. I smell money. Monday night. Fundamentalist's in-ring debut. He wins with The Koran Kick. Kabbalah Kick. Koran Kabbalah Kick.

CHAD DEITY. *(reappearing)* Um. KKK.

EKO. Yeah, KKK…oh, maybe not so good.

(**CHAD** *disappears.*)

I'll figure it out. Next week, The Fundamentalist makes his in-ring debut.

(**EKO**, **THE BAD GUY**, *and* **VP** *leave.*)

MACE. So, next week, The Fundamentalist's in-ring debut, I am as calm as I've ever been while walking into an arena. I am going to be a manager for the first time in my career, not a wrestler – all I need to do is walk The Fundamentalist down the aisle, jaw off with the crowd in my stupid fake accent, then raise my guy's hand in victory. Anything goes wrong, I'm there to clean up the mess.

And really, what could go wrong?

RING ANNOUNCER. The following contest is scheduled for one fall with a ten-minute time limit. Introducing first, from Hope, Arkansas, Billy Heartland.

(*THE BAD GUY enters as Billy Heartland, Americana to the extreme. His entrance, like all the entrances, is ridiculous.*)

MACE. Seriously. But Billy Heartland makes no difference to me, because he's a prop, a tool, an inanimate object that will be forgotten immediately after he is announced, because The Elaborate Entrance of The Fundamentalist is about to be all anyone could think about.

EKO. And his opponent…

(*It might be pretty awesome to have some version of The Fundamentalist's entrance actually happening as MACE describes it.*)

MACE. The lights in the arena dim.

Ten women in designer burkas line the entrance way.

A series of red and yellow streamers descend from the ceiling, no doubt referencing the obvious ties between this radical Islamist terrorist and Communist China.

The Fundamentalist's music begins, and as horribly offensive and culturally inaccurate as it is, it still makes my spine shiver in glee.

I appear first, lit cigar – Cuban, of course – in one hand, a little set of bongos hoisted above my head in the other.

Seriously. They give me a pair of bongos.

It doesn't matter.

I step aside, and there he is –

(VP appears as The Fundamentalist.)

– and I don't look back at him because I know he is exactly where he needs to be.

And it all goes by in a blur, because, for the first time, I am a part of an elaborate entrance instead of watching it from the perspective of the soon-to-be-vanquished.

(The Fundamentalist enters the ring.)

And the bell rings, and The Fundamentalist soaks up the boos of the fans, and, nah, he ain't The Fundamentalist, he's Vigneshwar Paduar. And the match starts, and Billy Heartland is playing his part...

(Billy Heartland plays his part.)

...and he's terrified of The Fundamentalist, and he's not sure what to make of it all, and it's the moment, the moment we've built for, and I look at Vigneshwar Paduar...and he doesn't fucking move.

(VP doesn't fucking move.)

Um.

He's not Vigneshwar Paduar right now. He's not even The Fundamentalist right now. He's...some guy.

He's some guy standing there in the ring. And he's not prepared to be there.

Something has gone wrong. And I'm supposed to clean up the mess.

So what do I do?

I jump up on the ring apron, lit cigar in one hand, bongo set in the other.

I yell frantically at poor Billy Heartland, calling him every mild anti-US name in the book, hoping that he'll follow my lead and catch the life preserver I'm tossing his way.

And the kid, he's acting his ass off, selling this like he's Amy Morton in *August: Osage County* –

(Pause. Oh, and feel free to change the reference to whatever local actor gave the most memorable recent performance.)

MACE. *(cont.)* What? Wrestlers can have culture.

So I'm watching the referee out of the corner of my eye, and he's just staring at VP, who is still locked, still looking at something that's not any of us.

And since the ref's back is turned, I take it as an opening, just like a real manager would do, were this a legitimate sporting event.

And when Poor Billy Heartland turns around, I slam the goddamn bongos against the flat of his back, just under his neck.

It's a good safe spot to hit someone who isn't expecting it.

Especially when you're dealing with foreign objects.

(to a specific audience member.)

Remind me to talk about foreign objects later.

And Poor Billy Heartland, God bless his soul even though I'm an atheist, he sells the bongo like he's been shot with a cannon, and he stumbles forward, he stumbles towards The Fundamentalist, who, shockingly, fortuitously, snaps out of his stupor –

(VP superkicks Billy Heartland.)

– and hits Billy Heartland with the single most beautiful superkick I have ever seen.

The crowd collectively gasps.

And VP freezes again.

Doesn't go for a cover.

Doesn't play to the crowd.

Freezes.

Again.

Poor Billy Heartland stays down.

Brilliant, Genius, Beautiful Billy Heartland.

He just stays down.

The referee calls for the bell.

The Fundamentalist has won his first match with one move.

(**VP**, *backstage.*)

VP. There are a lot of fucking people out there.

I don't know if I can do this.

MACE. I don't know if he can do this either. I don't mention it.

VP. What do you think EKO is going to say?

MACE. If I could, if I believed it, I'd tell Vigneshwar not to seek acceptance or absolution from the rich, powerful, traditional power structure that pays our checks, because we, as "people of color," as citizens of nation-states with rich cultural histories, we define our own success, and people like EKO, they don't understand that shit.

But I *don't* believe it.

Vigneshwar Paduar fucked up. And I have my moments of being all militant and feeling like a freedom fighter – and I don't mean this Chavez Castro version of militant freedom fighter – but if you don't do your job right, especially in this business, in my business, on my behalf? I'm not standing between you and the boss to take the tongue lashing.

And take a guess how he reacts.

No seriously, take a guess.

(**MACE** *interacts with the audience until he gets the response he's looking for.*)

Exactly. He loved it.

(**EKO**'s *office. Maybe* **EKO**'s *got a videotape of the superkick that he's watching over and over again throughout this.*)

EKO. That kick. That goddamn kick.

MACE. EKO mentions his boxer briefs again here. I'll spare you the details.

EKO. You know what I had the announcers call it?

The Sleeper Cell.

How perfect is that?

The Fucking Sleeper Fucking Cell.

MACE. Um. I don't get it.

EKO. Doesn't matter if you get it. It works.

Like this guy.

(*gestures to* **VP**)

He works. I don't get it, but he works.

The fans, they're eating it up. He intimidates his opponents, then BAM – he lays them out. Sleeper Cell. What a fucking name!

This is what we're gonna do with The Fundamentalist now, kid.

Minimalism.

It fits with the fucking caves, the fucking anti-technology blahblahblah.

I want you to do as little as possible in the ring.

You'll have the mysterious, annoying, manager guy on the outside, he'll rant and rave, he'll interfere, he'll do the, do the, do the –

MACE. Heavy lifting.

EKO. He'll do the heavy lifting. But you, Vigneshwar Paduar, you stay minimal and mysterious and don't let the audience have any idea what you're capable of.

By the time we put you in a match with Chad, I'm thinking like three weeks away on Pay Per View, they'll be dying to see what you're going to have in store. Just remember your game plan: nothing, nothing, Sleeper Cell.

(**EKO** *exits.*)

MACE. Surprising things to come out of that conversation – besides him liking the match, I mean:

1. He called VP by his name. His full name. And pronounced it right. I'm still not sure he's ever learned to pronounce Macedonio Guerra.

2. He's already planning a Pay Per View match between The Fundamentalist and Chad Deity. Pay Per View is a big deal – all the TV builds to the Pay Per View, and you put your best stuff on the Pay Per View, because

people are paying to view it, so you try to give them something to spend their money on. He thinks VP is ready for that?

And 3. The Sleeper Cell? Really?

Unsurprising things to come out of that conversation – there's really only one. *I'm* going to be doing the heavy lifting.

But I guess I don't mind, because I kind of like the heavy lifting. And VP gets the business, I'm not worried about that. So if the boss is showing more faith in him than he ever showed in me – hell, I should just shut my mouth and go along for the ride.

(pause)

But somehow, I've still got this sneaking suspicion that there's this whole other factor that needs to be looked out for.

(CHAD DEITY *nails* **VP** *with a chair.)*

(VP *falls to the ground.)*

MACE. *(to the audience member he spoke to earlier)* I thought I told you to remind me to talk about foreign objects.

CHAD DEITY. You know something, brother, when The Deity started wrestling, he had a bit of an ego. In those days, the old-timers had ways of teaching cocky newcomers a measure of respect for the business. The old-timer who taught Chad respect, he did it with his fist against my face, right above my eye, repeatedly. Busted me wide open. Knocked me silly.

And when he was done, and we got backstage, and they stitched me up on the spot, he reached his hand out to me – as my thirteen stitches were going in – and he said "Darnell, I won't do this again if you don't make me." And I ain't had stitches since.

(silence)

MACE. Darnell?

CHAD DEITY. Birth name. Darnell Deity.

(*to* **VP**)

You needed to be woken up. I figured I'd do it now with a chair before someone had to do it with thirteen stitches, mess up that pretty little face.

(**CHAD DEITY** *holds his hand out to* **VP**.)

(**VP** *does not shake it.*)

You froze out there.

VP. Nope. Minimalism.

CHAD DEITY. No. You froze.

VP. And you got a refrigerator that's bigger than my living room and a crisper that your son uses to chill his Barbies. The audience liked it.

CHAD DEITY. You know how Chad knows you froze?

Ooh – The Champ rhymed.

You didn't mention Chad Deity.

MACE. I look at VP and he looks at me and I can tell that he thinks Chad Deity is just being an egotist here, and on some level, well, yeah. But right now, the egotist happens to have a point.

CHAD DEITY. Weeks of promos, all you've been talking about is Chad Deity this, Chad Deity that, parading around one of the special limited edition Chad Deity posters that's now available out in the lobby.

You hate The Deity so much you spit in his metaphorical face.

And now...you don't so much as reference his name.

MACE. Shit.

I didn't even think of that, and it's my job to think of it.

I hope he doesn't mention it.

CHAD DEITY. And Mace, you didn't even think of it. It's your job to think of it.

MACE. Shit. He always mentions it.

VP. You know, Chad Deity, Vigneshwar Paduar appreciates Chad Deity's point, but The Fundamentalist seemed to get a pretty damn good response tonight without mentioning Chad Deity. Maybe The Fundamentalist just has new ideas to get the audience involved that Chad Deity is too old and set in Chad Deity's ways to even think of.

CHAD DEITY. You froze, Baby!

It's cool. It happens.

Next week, you need to mention Chad Deity.

Because to be honest with you, as soon as you decided to make the destruction of Chad Deity the only goal that your characters have, you wrote yourself into a short career.

Chad Deity's going to beat you.

And you're going to have nowhere left to go.

If you go out there next week, and you mention Chad Deity, and you wrestle a quick little match, and you hit that sweet superkick, we can at least extend this out a bit.

Maybe turn your vendetta against The Champ into something we can sell.

(pause)

You know, you remind Chad Deity...of Chad Deity.

(CHAD DEITY *exits.)*

(silence)

MACE. *(to* **VP***)* Um.

You know.

Nothing he said was exactly wrong.

VP. Everything he is is wrong.

If it wasn't for the respect I have for you, bro, I'd tell him exactly how wrong he is.

(VP *exits.)*

MACE. So...

(MACE *remembers where he left off.)*

Okay, right. So the following week, EKO pulls out a stop I thought would have been too obvious even for him.

RING ANNOUNCER. The following contest is scheduled for one fall with a ten-minute time limit. Introducing first, from Main Street, USA…this is Old Glory!

(**THE BAD GUY,** *in an American flag mask, as Old Glory.*)

MACE. I work in a subtle business.

RING ANNOUNCER. And his opponent…

(**VP,** *as The Fundamentalist*)

MACE. The Fundamentalist's entrance is just a touch more elaborate this week than last.

Twenty women in burkas line the entrance way.

The red and yellow streamers are joined by indechiperable (and probably pure gibberish) Sanskrit spelled out in green laser in the center of the ring.

On the walk down the aisle, I sneak a look back at VP, and from the intensity in his eyes, I can see that he's determined to redeem himself. He's destined for glory, finally.

(*He gestures to Old Glory.*)

Destined for "Glory" – forget it.

The Fundamentalist gets to the ring, and he prays, and Che Chavez Castro curses out the fans in Spanish, cause all I know in Spanish is the curses, and the bell rings, and Old Glory does his part, he plays to the crowd and starts a USA USA chant –

(*Old Glory plays to the crowd.*)

– and this, this guy, this menace, this, this…Fundamentalist is terrifying, and he's just staring at Old Glory, and he's not moving, and…

Ah fuck. Vigneshwar Paduar has frozen again.

(*Old Glory throws up his hands in disgust.*)

Now, Old Glory is no Billy Heartland. Old Glory is a legitimate old school tough guy reared in a different era, an era in which if a young whippersnapper dishonored the craft – if he took something without giving back – it was up to the old-timers to give him a *receipt.*

A *potato.* Thirteen stitches. Old Glory wants permission to beat Vigneshwar Paduar's ass.

At this point, that sounds like a really good fucking plan to me.

So I give him the subtlest of gestures, and Old Glory, instead of coming to jaw with The Fundamentalist's manager the way Poor Billy Heartland did, makes his move. He approaches cautiously, still giving the impression that The Fundamentalist is one to be feared, but I know that Old Glory is about to put some serious hurt on –

(The Fundamentalist superkicks Old Glory.)

The audience gasps.

Old Glory later tells me that he was knocked cold legit.

The Fundamentalist does not go for a pin.

The referee assumes that we're following the same game plan as last week, and declares the match over.

The Fundamentalist has won his first two matches with a total of two – count 'em – two wrestling moves. And they were both the same move.

(Che Chavez Castro raises The Fundamentalist's hand in victory. The Fundamentalist yanks his hand away.)

(MACE and **VP** stare each other down. **MACE** regains his composure.)

But now's not the time to berate him for what he's done.

I've got work to do.

As the bell rings, I grab a microphone and join my man in the squared circle.

I'm going to be cutting a promo from the ring.

The goal of this promo is clear to me.

We hate Chad Deity.

The Fundamentalist hates Chad Deity.

Che Chavez Castro hates Chad Deity.

And what I'm going to do is make sure everyone in the audience knows it –

(VP grabs the microphone away.)

VP. *(as The Fundamentalist)* The Fundamentalist hates America.

MACE. The Fundamentalist is not supposed to speak.

VP. The Fundamentalist hates Old Glory.

The Fundamentalist hates Billy Heartland.

The Fundamentalist hates The New York City.

(And of course, change that last line to fit your hometown or beloved local monument.)

MACE. And even here, at this point, I can tell that this is going to go very, very wrong.

And it does.

VP. The Fundamentalist hates...

MACE. The Fundamentalist announces a long list of everyone and everything that he hates. Conspicuous by its absence, as the late Gorilla Monsoon used to say, is the name of Chad Deity.

VP. The Fundamentalist hates expensive refrigerators. The Fundamentalist hates raisin bread.

MACE. He's showing off, but it's worse than showing off, cause it's just for people behind the scenes, and it's just to show that he can, to show that he knows what he's expected to do, and to make it clear that he's not interested in doing it.

He's being a dick.

VP. The Fundamentalist hates...THE Wrestling.

MACE. Vigneshwar Paduar just Sleeper Celled us both out of the main event.

The interview ends.

We get backstage.

(EKO and CHAD DEITY enter.)

The Boss and The Champ are waiting for us.

And they're just staring.

I can tell what they're about to do, and it's the right thing.

Call off the Pay Per View match.

Give VP a few more weeks to work with me on his respect for the business, on taking care of the guy he's in there with.

I'm glad they're here, cause they're saving me the hassle of having to handle the situation myself.

They look pissed.

This is gonna be good.

EKO. There he is – my next THE Champion.

MACE. I should just stop attempting to narrate, right?

EKO. The kicks, they're money. The fans, they love it. You hear it. You never hear reactions like that.

MACE. He's right.

The reactions are amazing. So are the superkicks.

EKO. And now, now's the time, now's the time when we make ourselves a small fortune. You see, kid, I created this little theory I call the rule of three.

MACE. Everett K. Olson did not create the rule of three.

EKO. Sleeper Cell to Billy Heartland, that's one. Sleeper Cell to Old Glory, that's two. You're making your way through the soul of these United States, kid. The fans, they know there's a third Sleeper Cell on the way.

CHAD DEITY. And the promo.

EKO. Oh, kid. The promo.

CHAD DEITY. Chad's gotta admit, the promo was brilliant.

MACE. He thought the promo was brilliant?

CHAD DEITY. The Champ told you that the only thing you needed to do was mention his name –

EKO. And you didn't even have to.

CHAD DEITY. Rule of Three.

The fans know that that third Sleeper Cell can only be meant for Chad Deity.

(CHAD takes off his championship belt.)

When I started out in THE Wrestling, the E to the K to the O told me that throwing money in the air was the stupidest idea he had ever heard.

EKO. I underestimated the champ.

CHAD DEITY. And now I underestimated the V to the motherfucking P.

(**CHAD** *hands the belt to* **VP.**)

Hold on to this for a little while.

You should get used to carrying it.

VP. So you liked it? That? You liked that?

EKO. Kid. I don't like things. Liking is not good for business. I do what's good for business. Right now, giving you the belt is what's good for business. We're gonna make millions from folks dying to see Chad Deity try to get his title back and set things right with the world.

(*to* **MACE**)

Get him ready.

Next week, we put the title on The Fundamentalist.

(*silence*)

VP. That? They liked that?

(**VP** *drops the championship belt in disgust and exits.*)

(*silence*)

MACE. Okay.

So Vigneshwar Paduar – nah, revision – The Fundamentalist is about to become THE Champion.

He's fought two matches.

He knows one move.

I should be pissed, right?

I should be complaining about the fact that he goes out there, almost breaks the jaw of a respected veteran, cuts a promo completely disrespecting the business that I love, walks to the back and gets rewarded with the announcement of his first World Championship.

And I'm not gonna lie. There's a part of me that's infuriated by this.

But I don't know.

Maybe I take things too seriously.

I mean, Saturday morning, corn flakes and sugar –
maybe I've got this business all built up in my head.
Maybe I forget we're just wrestling guys.
We're just action figures. Just dolls.
Maybe I should just keep my mouth shut and make it
work.

(silence)

And I'm also not gonna lie.

(**MACE** *looks at the belt.*)

(**MACE** *walks to the belt.*)

(**MACE** *picks up the belt.*)

I never expected to get this close to championship gold.

(**MACE** *holds the belt up to his waist.*)

(silence)

(He likes the way it looks.)

(He really likes the way it looks.)

(He gets lost in the moment.)

*(He wonders what his grandfather would say if he saw
him like this.)*

(**MACE** *snaps out of it.*)

Shit. Sorry. I forgot I'm supposed to be telling a story.
So my job now is to get The Fundamentalist ready to
win the THE Championship –

(**VP** *nails* **MACE** *with a superkick to the jaw, out of
nowhere.*)

(**MACE** *goes down like he was shot.*)

VP. I'm going back to Brooklyn.

MACE. The shot that knocks you out is the one you never
see coming.

VP. I mean, look. You and me, we got stories to tell, and
they're different, but they come from the same place,
man – there's beauty in that. That's what I came here
to do.

VP. *(cont.)* But they want to turn us, they want to spin our story, fit us in to what they already got in mind. Chad Deity is Chad Deity. I don't want to be The Fundamentalist. You don't want to be Che Chavez Castro.

And if we go along with it, no matter how we play it, if it's bad and fucked up, or if we sneak in some good and sneak in something to say, we gotta go back to Brooklyn, back to the Bronx, we gotta look little brown kids in the eye and defend our decision, we gotta explain why it ain't so bad to exist outside ourselves for the sake of twenty pounds of gold around our waist.

MACE. *(to VP)* That's bullshit. You're scared.

(to the audience)

And it just slips out of my mouth.

VP. Maybe. But am I wrong?

(no response)

I didn't come here to be champion, man.

I came to create something dope.

And I think we did as much we can.

(no response)

And I know that I'm wrong here, I should just be like you, and keep my mouth shut and make it work. But when I see something's wrong, I gotta say something. I gotta do something. I gotta solve it.

*(**MACE** goes to speak.)*

*(**VP** superkicks **MACE** again – sudden, shocking, laying **MACE** out flat.)*

This is how I know to solve this. It was good working with you, bro.

*(**VP** exits.)*

(silence)

*(**CHAD DEITY** rushes in to **MACE**'s side.)*

(He helps him to his feet.)

(**EKO** *enters.*)

EKO. Where's your boy, Mace?

(*no response*)

Where. Is your boy. Mace?

(*no response*)

He's under contract.
As are you.

CHAD DEITY. It's not his fault, Everett.

EKO. You're under contract too, *Darnell.*

(*silence*)

CHAD DEITY. Sorry, Mace.

(**CHAD DEITY** *reluctantly turns on* **MACE,** *clotheslining him to the ground.*)

(**THE BAD GUY** *enters, carrying the Che Chavez Castro costume.*)

EKO. You are an important part of THE Wrestling, Macedonio Guerra.
You make this business run.
I respect you.

(**CHAD DEITY** *pulls* **MACE** *to his feet.*)

(**EKO** *holds out his hand.*)

(**MACE** *reluctantly shakes it.*)

(**EKO** *holds onto* **MACE** *'s hand.*)

But right now, I have a problem. And that problem is your fault. So I'm going to need you to get out there and solve my problem.

(*silence*)

(**MACE** *takes the costume.*)

(**MACE** *does not move.*)

I said. Get out there. And solve. My –

(**MACE** *punches* **EKO.**)

(silence)

(**MACE** *physically fights to be heard as he finally says what he has desperately needed to say for so long.*)

MACE. And I mention it, I mention it all –

Everett K. Olson did not invent professional wrestling and I'm not okay with pretending that he did and ignoring the long, rich history of the art form of professional wrestling that existed long before he ever even dreamed of THE Wrestling, and yeah, I said art form, because that's what this is about, working together to make something beautiful, and it's not about Chad Deity's muscles and money and elaborate entrance, and Chad Deity's muscles and money and elaborate entrance do not represent my American Dream, because my American Dream roots for the underdog, my American Dream respects hard work and substance and throwing your life into doing what you love just like my grandpa taught me in 1986 –

– and before I know it I'm sweating and spitting and crying, and I mention all of it, I mention the money and I mention Cruger Avenue, 10:45am, I mention my brother and my brother and my grandpa and the shit sugar water and the shit wrestling guys and the shit the fucking shit –

– and I mention how easy it would be for Everett K. Olson and Chad Deity and Vigneshwar fucking Paduar to get the fuck out of my way and let me tell a story, a perfect goddamn story and I mention all this, a story, a perfect goddamn story is all I have ever desired in my existence, and they could keep the money and the power and the prestige and I would do every last bit of the heavy motherfucking lifting if they would just let me tell One. Perfect. Goddamn. Story.

(silence)

(**MACE** *stands over a stunned* **EKO, CHAD DEITY,** *and* **THE BAD GUY.***)*

(**MACE** *realizes what he has done.*)

(**EKO** *approaches* **MACE** *threataningly.*)

EKO. Do that on television.

(silence)

MACE. So I do.

End of Act Two

EPILOGUE

(VIGNESHWAR PADUAR.)

VP. I turn on my television this night, of all nights, and I flick the channels, and there's THE Wrestling.

My job a week ago.

Probably still my job now, if you want to get all legal about it.

(EKO *enters. On TV.*)

And the first face I see, maybe no surprise, is the boss.

EKO. On behalf of THE Wrestling, and on behalf of THE Champion Chad Deity, I would like to condemn the comments –

VP. And I'm watching with a girl, cause I'm, you know, me, and I'm watching with a girl, and the wrestling comes on and she rolls her eyes.

She gets up and breaks for the bathroom, smooshing my face playful, telling me that when she gets back, we best be watching something more real.

(MACE *enters as Che Chavez Castro.*)

The Fundamentalist should be standing there, staring through the camera, indefinable menace that's, for honest, kinda cool to the folks who pay their cash to boo indefinable menaces.

But he's not.

Che Chavez Castro is.

Alone.

And he's staring.

And he ain't saying nothing.

And for me, reading his eyes is easy.

Cause I put it there.

VP. *(cont.)* I put there the hope and the idealism, the sense that, fuck, we could change some world through this.

I put there the contempt and the disgust, the abandonment and the distrust and the sense that, fuck, the people on your own side of the struggle can't be counted on to soldier through.

Especially if they got a little cash.

Or a gas station.

Or luxury lofts.

*(**MACE** begins to remove the Che Chavez Castro costume.)*

And then I don't know what he's doing.

The costume's coming off.

And he's still not speaking.

He's still staring, at me, at Everett K. EKO Olson, at Chad Darnell Deity, at Brooklyn, at The Bronx, at probably Kansas and Montana, at every small city and big town and every thirteen-year-old kid sitting at his kitchen counter doing homework during the commercials, and that's not no Mexican radical revolutionary fascist liberal dictator guerrilla freedom-hating freedom fighter.

That's my boy Mace.

*(**MACE** does not speak.)*

And he speaks.

He speaks calm.

He speaks slow.

He speaks out of character.

He speaks as Macedonio Guerra.

*(**MACE** does not speak.)*

And the girl, she comes back in the room.

I had forgot her.

She asks "we're still watching this?"

*(**MACE** does not speak.)*

And I think about it.

VP. *(cont.)* And I stand up, and I kiss her perfect on the lips, then again on the cheek, and I smile wide, and I might have done the same thing last time she was here, cause I'm, you know, me, but right now this time, I'm not trying to get in her pants.

And I tell her to just listen.

And she listens.

And we watch.

And Macedonio Guerra goes ahead and gives voice to our little corner of the world.

(CHAD DEITY enters. No elaborate entrance.)

And when he's done, Chad Deity comes out.

And they stare down.

And they stand off.

And the referee rings the bell.

(MACE and CHAD DEITY do not move.)

And we watch

Live via satellite

From someplace in the heart of THE United States as

To the cheers of an ecstatic throng

(CHAD DEITY powerbombs MACE.)

Chad Deity

Defeats

Macedonio Guerra

In near-record time.

The crowd goes wild.

(MACE exits through the audience, almost unnoticed, as CHAD DEITY celebrates, the conquering hero.)

And the girl, she turns to me, and she says:

Why are they rooting for the bad guy?

(VP exits.)

(CHAD celebrates. For a long time.)

(blackout)

End of Play

OTHER TITLES AVAILABLE FROM SAMUEL FRENCH

STUNNING

David Adjmi

Drama / 2m, 4f / Unit Set

Sixteen year-old Lily knows nothing beyond the Syrian-Jewish community in Brooklyn where she lives a cloistered life with her much older husband. Soon an unlikely relationship with her enigmatic African-American maid opens Lily's world to new possibilities – but at a huge price. David Adjmi's daring new work shifts from caustic satire to violent drama as it exposes the ways we invent and defend our identities in the melting-pot of America.

David Adjmi received the first ever Steinberg "Mimi" Playwright Award in 2009.

"Impossible to dismiss...An artist...whose next work
I can't wait to see."
– Hilton Als, *The New Yorker*

"Virtuosic playwright David Adjmi nicely evokes an arrestingly skewed subculture onstage...coolly witty...A stinging portrait of an insular Syrian Jewish community in contemporary Brooklyn."
– Jason Zinoman, *The New York Times*

"Unless you happen to live in an insular Syrian-Jewish community, the culture shock of *Stunning* could be quite...well, stunning. David Adjmi's eye-opening drama about a despotic rag merchant, his tyrannized child bride and the black maid who challenges the medieval customs of their domestic life has a chilling impact. Riveting performances and super-stylish staging polish the play's satirical weapons of high dudgeon, while adding to the luster of LCT3, the developmental wing of Lincoln Center currently making a splash in its inaugural season at the Duke."
– Marilyn Stasio, *Variety*

OTHER TITLES AVAILABLE FROM SAMUEL FRENCH

A STEADY RAIN

Keith Huff

Drama / 2m / Bare Stage

A dark duologue filled with sharp storytelling and biting repartee, *A Steady Rain* explores the complexities of a lifelong bond tainted by domestic affairs, violence, and the rough streets of Chicago. Joey and Denny have been best friends since kindergarten, and after working together for several years as policemen in Chicago, they are practically family: Joey helps out with Denny's wife and kids; Denny keeps Joey away from the bottle. But when a domestic disturbance call takes a turn for the worse, their friendship is put on the line. The result is a harrowing journey into a moral gray area where trust and loyalty struggle for survival against a sobering backdrop of pimps, prostitutes, and criminal lowlifes.

"Keith Huff's *A Steady Rain* offers one of the most powerful theatrical experiences in many seasons."
–David Sheward, *Back Stage*

"Characteristic of Chicagoland theater at its gritty, no-nonsense best...An irresistibly forceful exercise in noir-style tandem storytelling."
– Terry Teachout, *The Wall Street Journal*

"A gritty, rich, thick, poetic and entirely gripping noir tale of two Chicago police officers whose inner need to serve and protect both consumes them and rips them apart."
– Chris Jones, *Chicago Tribune*

"Huff's vivid, intricately layered script...lifts [the play] far above the usual clichés, both detaching us from the melodrama and imbuing it with the force of tragedy."
– Richard Zoglin, *Time*